For Juan

The King and His Friends

by Jose Aruego

Charles Scribner's Sons
New York

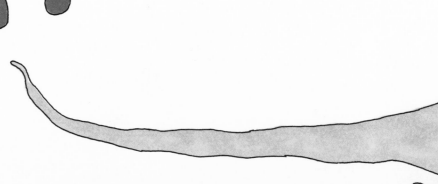

King Doowah had three friends—two dragons and a griffin. The friends played many games and did everything they could to amuse their king.

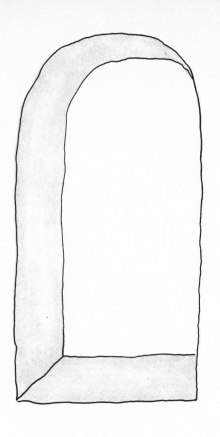

Wherever the king went in the castle, his friends joined him in a parade. The griffin fluttered over his head, and the dragons trotted on either side as the king walked proudly between them.

Best of all, the king loved decorations, and luckily
his friends could decorate anything. Indeed, the huge
castle would have been a plain and gloomy place if
they had not entertained themselves and the king

by decorating the throne,
a bookstand, a mirror . . .

The friends adorned each door in many beautiful ways. The king picked the cleverest decoration before entering.

The dragons puffed glimmering sparks to light the dark passages. The griffin carried the king's train to prevent it from getting dirty.

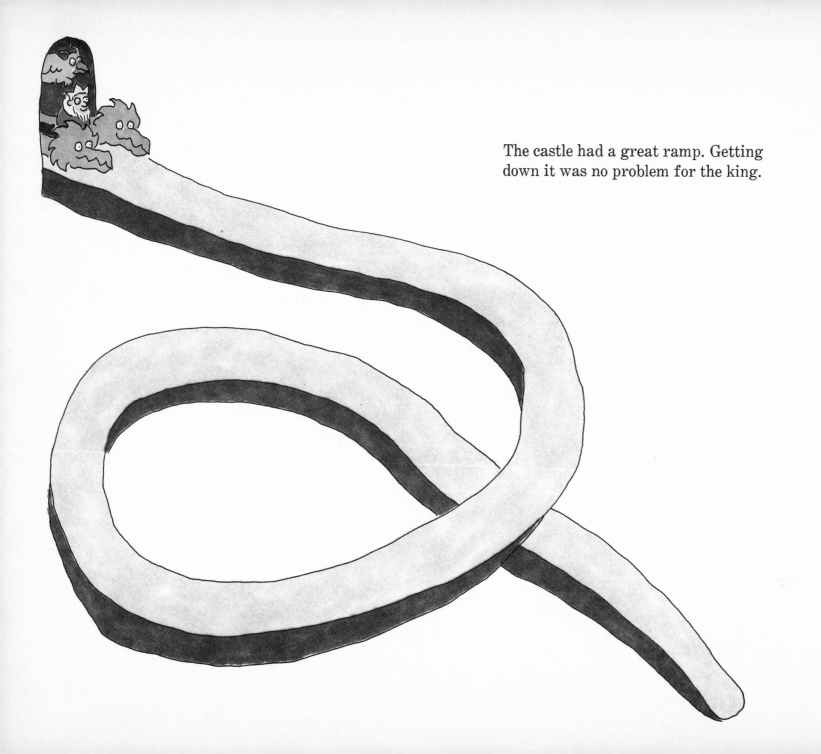

The castle had a great ramp. Getting
down it was no problem for the king.

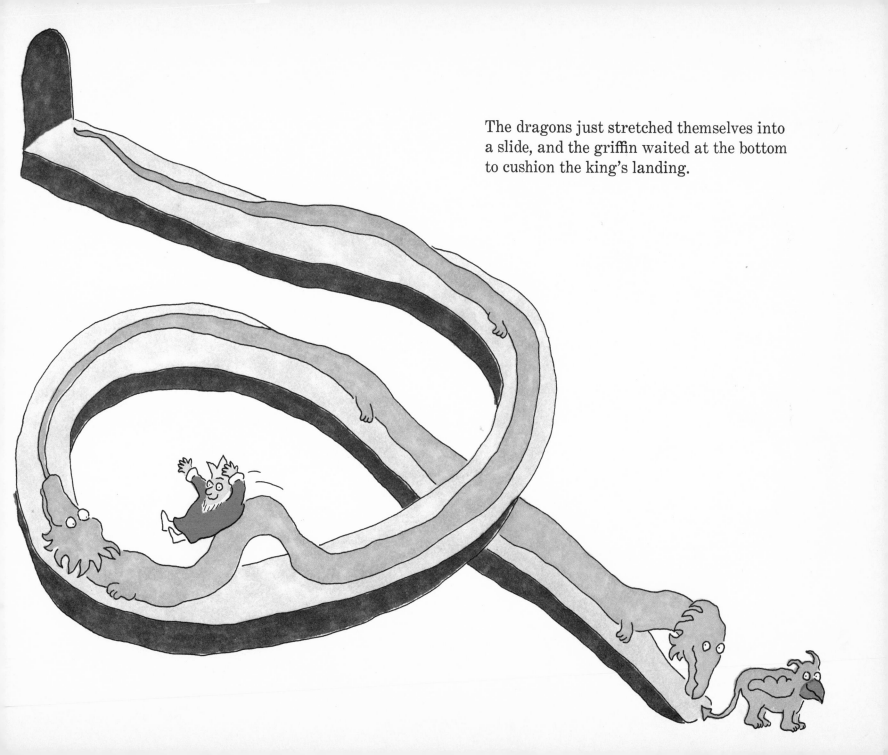

The dragons just stretched themselves into a slide, and the griffin waited at the bottom to cushion the king's landing.

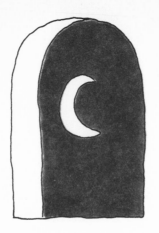

At bedtime, when the king got sleepy, the griffin carried him to his chamber. The dragons draped themselves around the bed while the griffin made a canopy with his wings. The minute the king fell asleep, his friends hopped into bed beside him.

On nice days the friends got up at dawn. They liked to spend the day in the forest, enjoying themselves and searching for adventure. Something always happened in the forest.

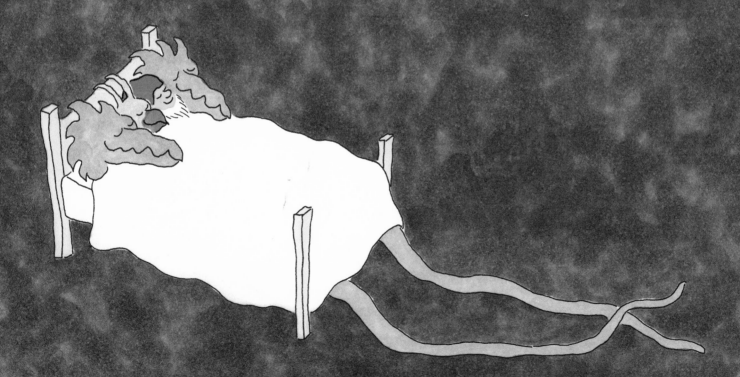

First they went to their favorite glen, where the dragons roasted chestnuts for breakfast. Everyone ate too many, so they rested.

Then they played games. The king threw sticks
for the griffin and dragons to chase.

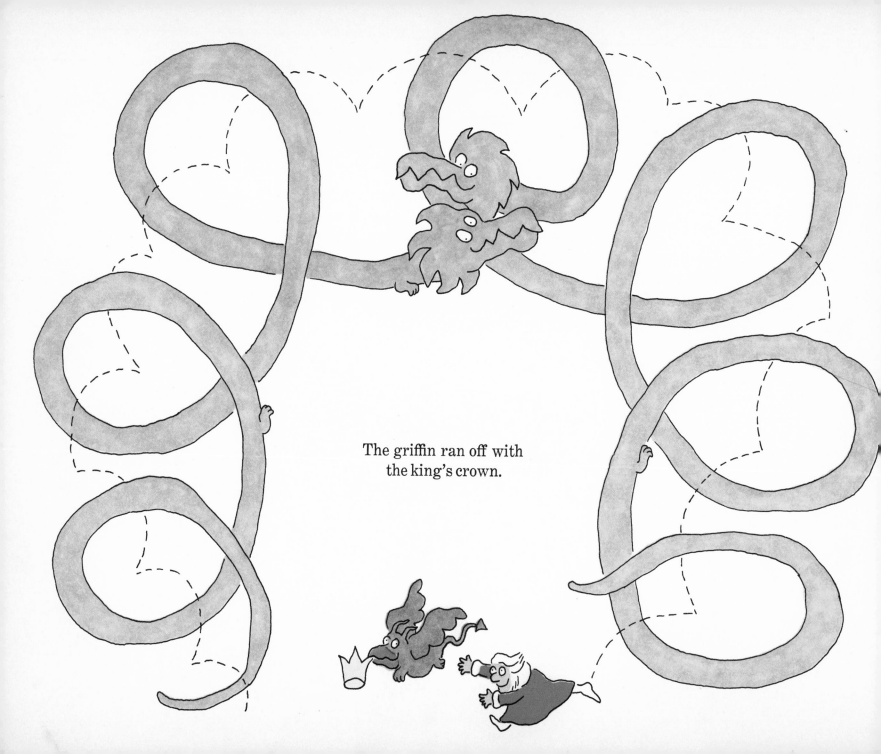

The griffin ran off with
the king's crown.

They stopped to admire their reflections in a clear pool.
What they saw was an eight-eyed, fantastic beast.

One day as they were walking in the forest, they
were startled by a low, pounding noise and saw clouds
of dust rising in the distance.

The king took hold of a dragon with each hand, the griffin gently lifted the king by his robe and then flew them over to take a closer look. They saw a stampeding herd of unicorns heading straight towards the edge of a cliff.

The friends knew they must act quickly to save the unicorns. The king had a plan. He sent the griffin to find a very tall tree.

The griffin flew high to look in all directions.

He soon found the tallest tree in the forest and hurried back to his friends to carry them to it.

The dragons blew their flames
full force to fell the tree.
The griffin pushed.

Working together down the length of the tree trunk, the dragons burned off half the wood to make a tremendous log with one flat side.

The log was very heavy, but finally, with everybody hanging on,
the griffin was able to lift it, and they flew to the rescue.

When the friends reached the unicorns,
the herd was about to go over the edge.

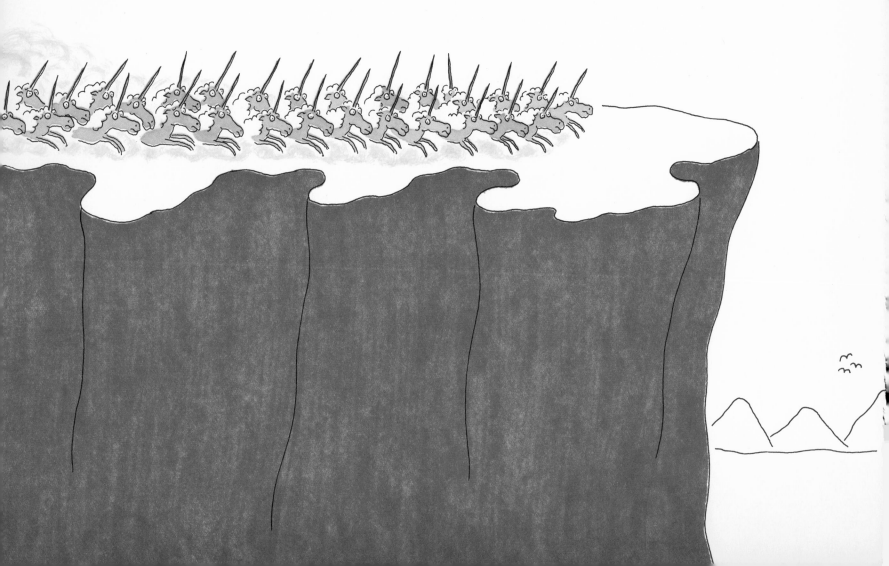

The friends flew directly over the herd and dropped the log. The unicorns raised their horns to protect themselves from being crushed.

Their sharp horns pierced the wood and its weight made them stop. The unicorns trembled with fear when they saw how close they had come to falling off the cliff.

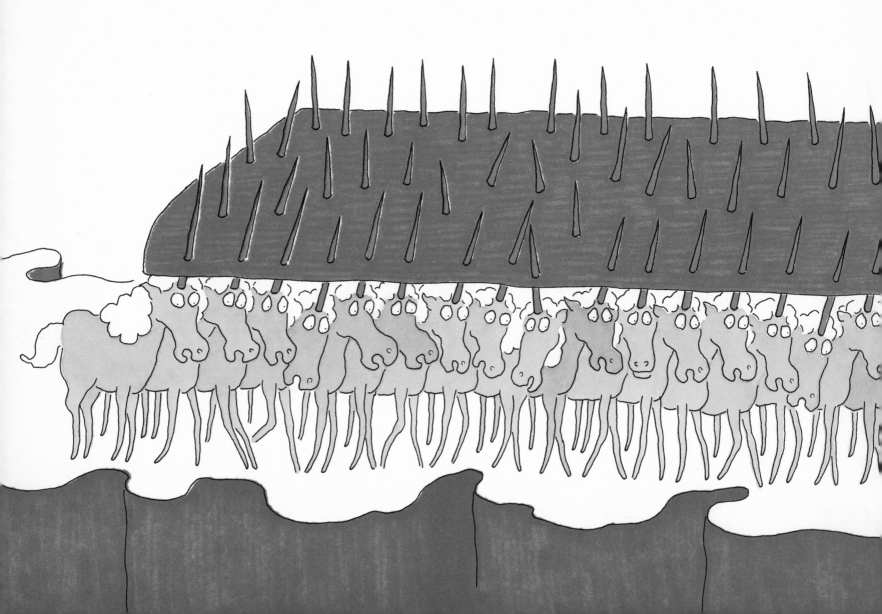

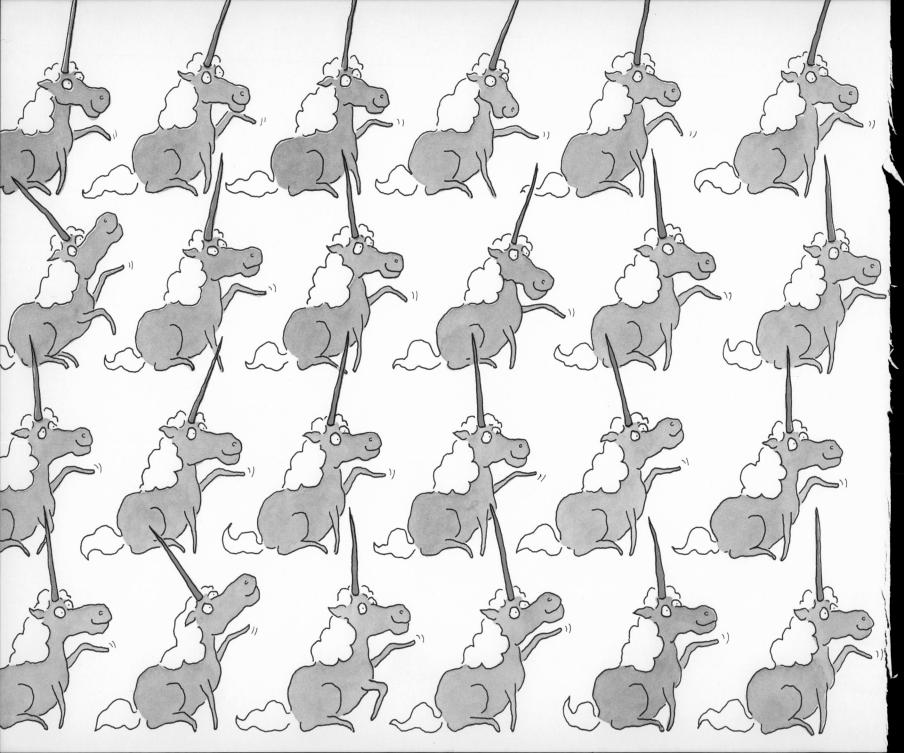

The dragons removed the log. The unicorns thanked the king
and his friends and promised never again to run blindly after
each other without thinking of where they were going. This made
the king glad, and he invited the unicorns to visit the castle
anytime. Everyone waved good-bye as the king and his friends
took the log back to the castle as a trophy.

The king had it hung over the mantelpiece to remind them of their adventure. From then on, the castle was a lively place, for there were always some unicorns visiting the king and his friends.